FEB 1 2 2019

GUARDIANS OF THE GALAXY

ROCKET RACCOON™ #1

A CHASING TALE PART ONE

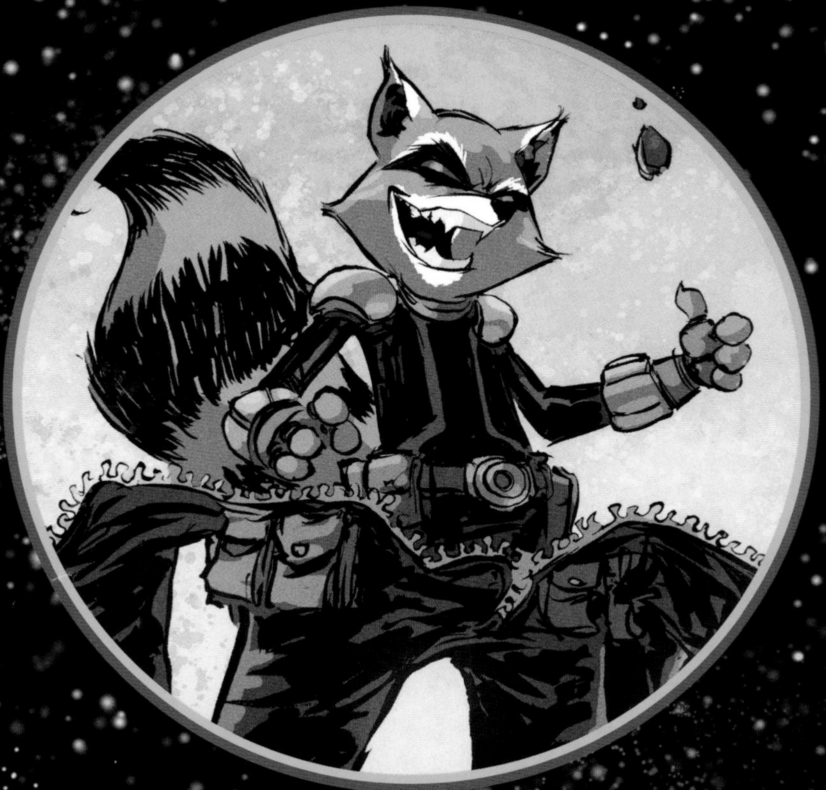

MARVEL
marvelkids.com

ABDO Spotlight

ABDOPUBLISHING.COM

Reinforced library bound edition published in 2018 by Spotlight,
a division of ABDO, PO Box 398166, Minneapolis, Minnesota 55439.
Spotlight produces high-quality reinforced library bound editions for
schools and libraries. Published by agreement with Marvel Characters, Inc.

Printed in the United States of America, North Mankato, Minnesota.
042017
092017

THIS BOOK CONTAINS
RECYCLED MATERIALS

marvelkids.com
© 2017 MARVEL

PUBLISHER'S CATALOGING IN PUBLICATION DATA

Names: Young, Skottie, author. | Young, Skottie ; Beaulieu, Jean-Francois ; Parker,
Jake, illustrators.
Title: Rocket Raccoon / writer: Skottie Young ; art: Skottie Young ; Jean-Francois
Beaulieu ; Jake Parker.
Description: Reinforced library bound edition. | Minneapolis, Minnesota : Spotlight,
2018. | Series: Guardians of the galaxy : Rocket Raccoon | Volumes 1, 2, 3, and
4 written by Skottie Young ; illustrated by Skottie Young & Jean-Francois
Beaulieu. | Volumes 5 and 6 written by Skottie Young ; illustrated by Skottie
Young , Jake Parker & Jean-Francois Beaulieu.
Summary: Rocket's high-flying life of adventure is at stake when he's framed for
murder, and with an imposter one step ahead of him, and various terminators
tracking him, can Rocket make it out alive and clear his name?
Identifiers: LCCN 2017931597 | ISBN 9781532140846 (#1: A Chasing Tale Part
One) | ISBN 9781532140853 (#2: A Chasing Tale Part Two) | ISBN
9781532140860 (#3: A Chasing Tale Part Three) | ISBN 9781532140877 (#4: A
Chasing Tale Part Four) | ISBN 9781532140884 (#5: Storytailer) | ISBN
9781532140891 (#6: Misfit Mechs)
Subjects: LCSH: Superheroes--Juvenile fiction. | Adventure and adventurers--
Juvenile fiction. | Comic books, strips, etc.--Juvenile fiction. | Graphic novels--
Juvenile fiction.
Classification: DDC 741.5--dc23
LC record available at https://lccn.loc.gov/2017931597

Spotlight

A Division of ABDO
abdopublishing.com

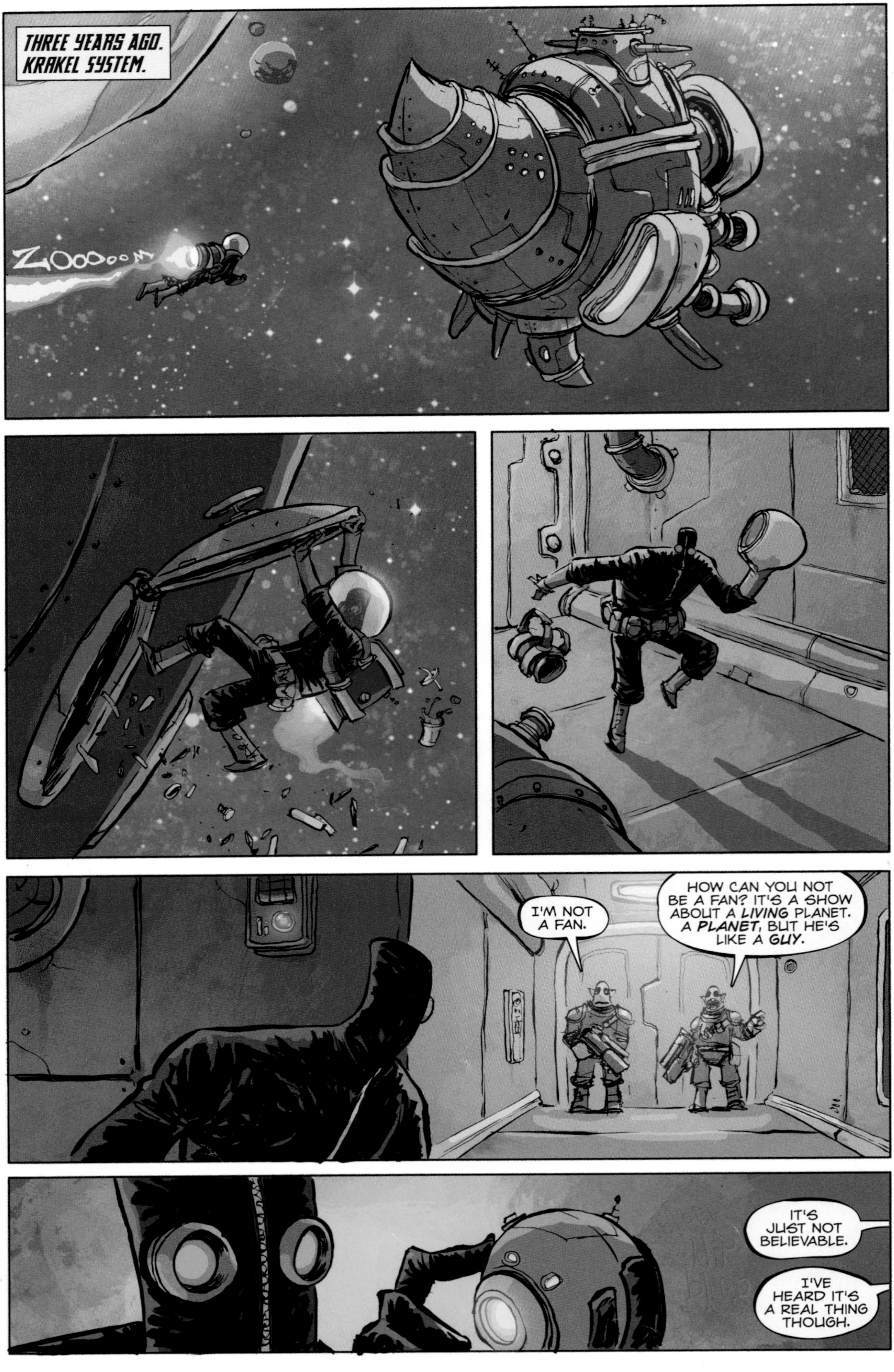
THREE YEARS AGO.
KRAKEL SYSTEM.
ZOOOoom
I'M NOT A FAN.
HOW CAN YOU NOT BE A FAN? IT'S A SHOW ABOUT A LIVING PLANET. A PLANET, BUT HE'S LIKE A GUY.
IT'S JUST NOT BELIEVABLE.
I'VE HEARD IT'S A REAL THING THOUGH.

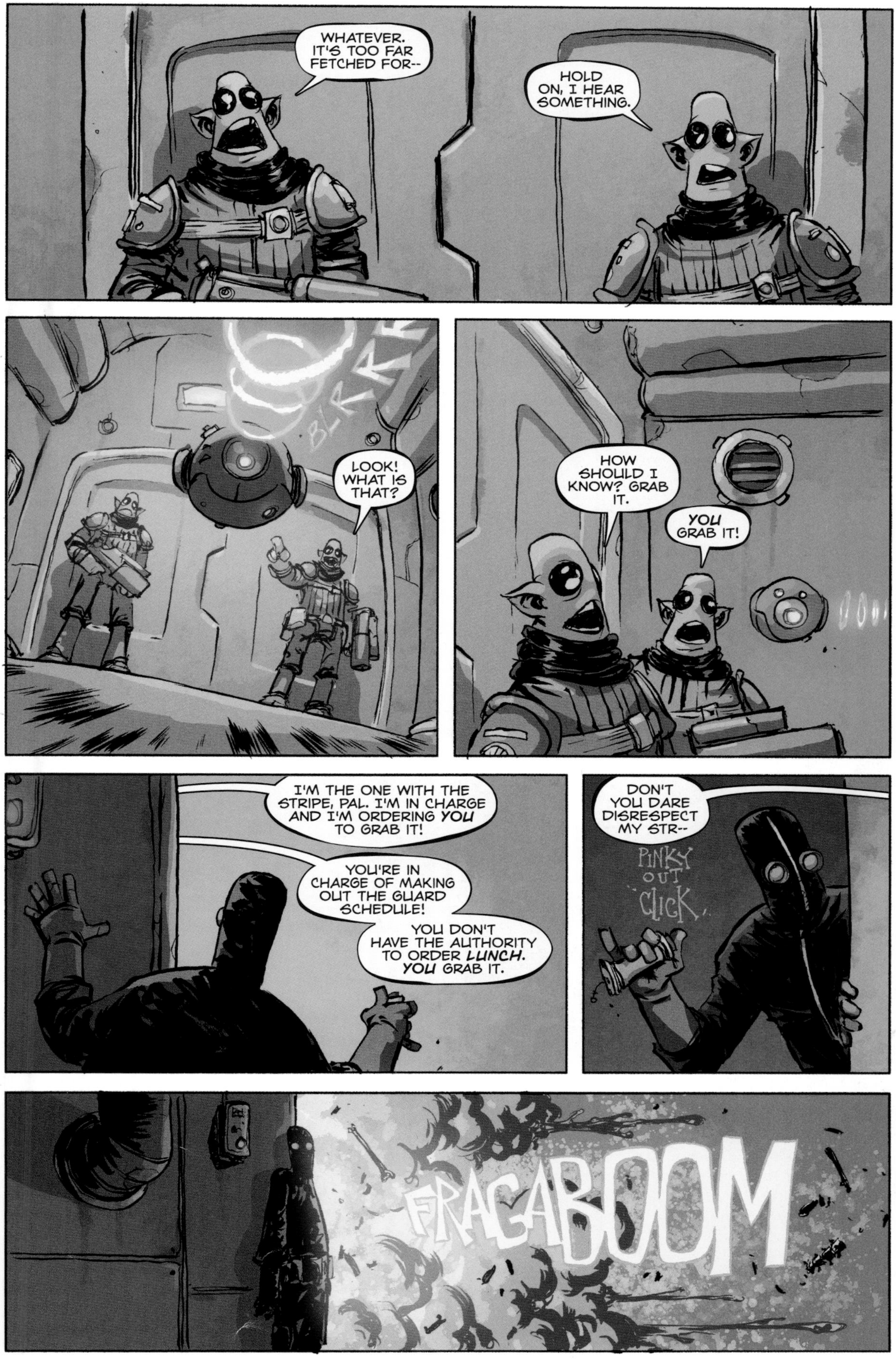
WHATEVER. IT'S TOO FAR FETCHED FOR--
HOLD ON, I HEAR SOMETHING.
BLRRR
LOOK! WHAT IS THAT?
HOW SHOULD I KNOW? GRAB IT.
YOU GRAB IT!
I'M THE ONE WITH THE STRIPE, PAL. I'M IN CHARGE AND I'M ORDERING YOU TO GRAB IT!
YOU'RE IN CHARGE OF MAKING OUT THE GUARD SCHEDULE!
YOU DON'T HAVE THE AUTHORITY TO ORDER LUNCH. YOU GRAB IT.
DON'T YOU DARE DISRESPECT MY STR--
PINKY OUT CLICK
FRAGABOOM

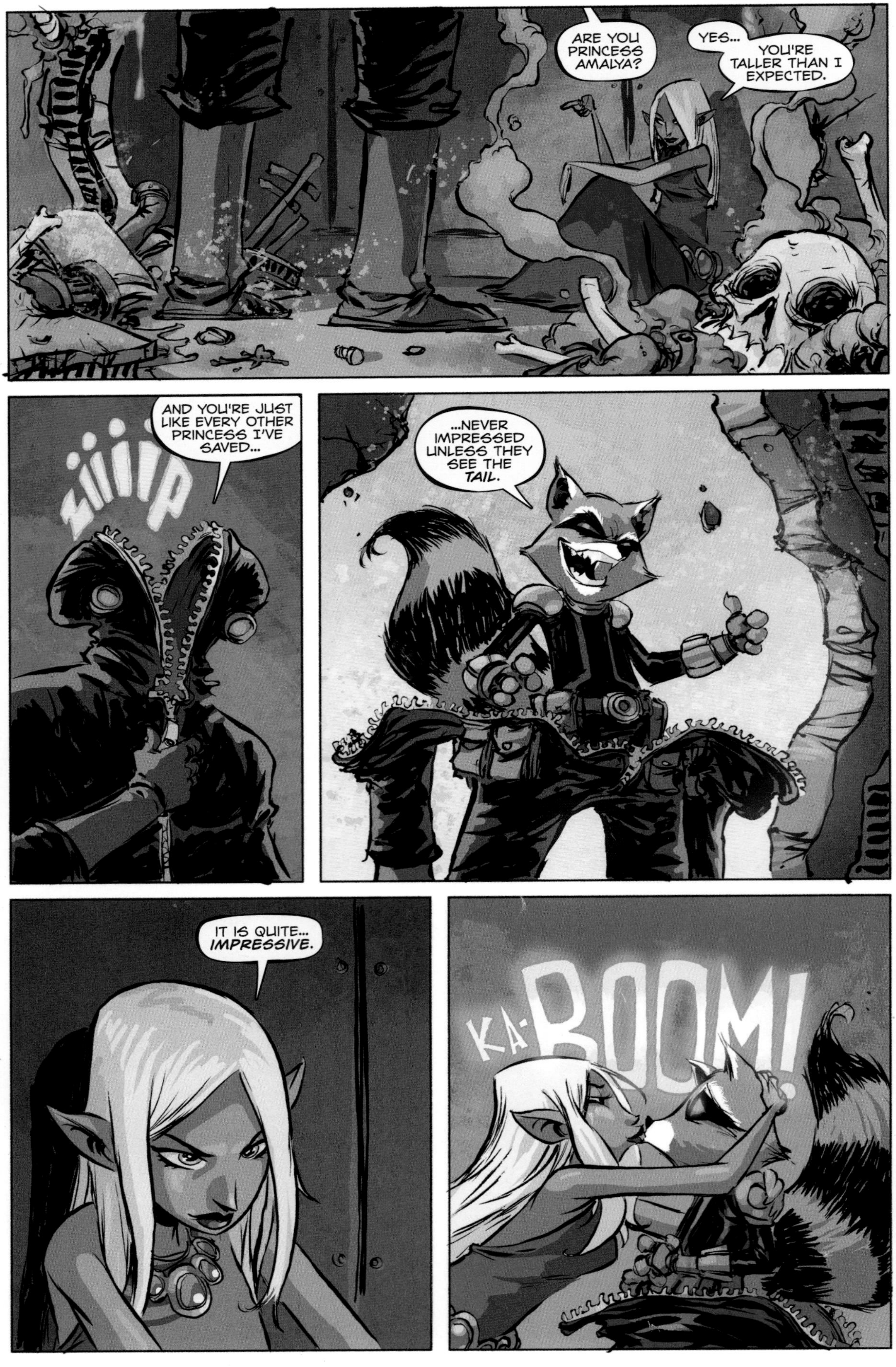
ARE YOU PRINCESS AMALYA?
YES... YOU'RE TALLER THAN I EXPECTED.
AND YOU'RE JUST LIKE EVERY OTHER PRINCESS I'VE SAVED...
ZIIIIP
...NEVER IMPRESSED UNLESS THEY SEE THE TAIL.
IT IS QUITE... IMPRESSIVE.
KA-BOOM!

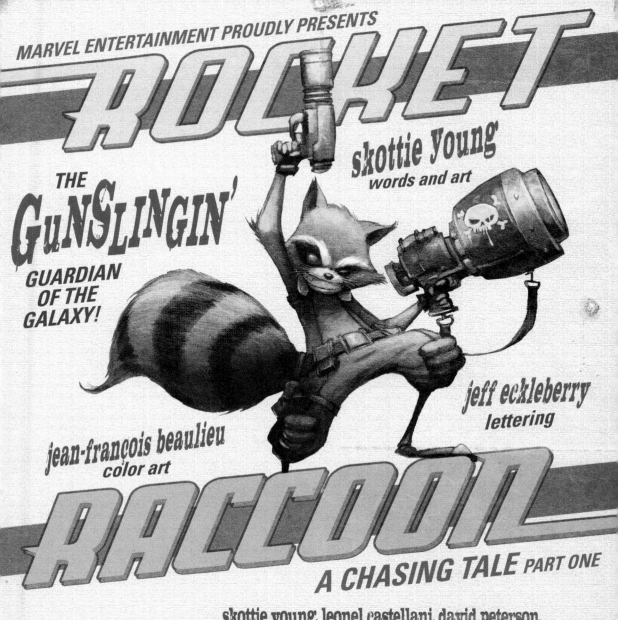

MARVEL ENTERTAINMENT PROUDLY PRESENTS

ROCKET RACCOON

THE GUNSLINGIN' GUARDIAN OF THE GALAXY!

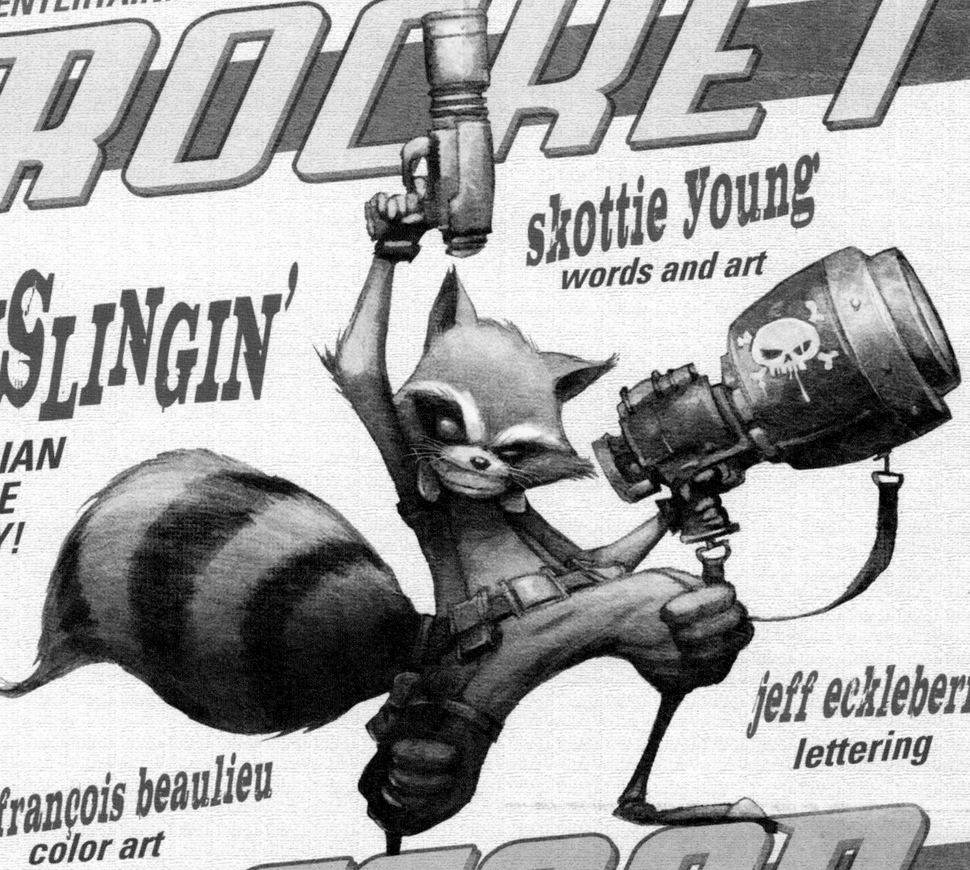

skottie young
words and art

jeff eckleberry
lettering

jean-françois beaulieu
color art

A CHASING TALE PART ONE

skottie young
cover art

skottie young, leonel castellani, david peterson, j. scott campbell & nei ruffino, sara pichelli & justin ponsor, jeff smith & tom gaadt, dale keown & jason keith
variant covers

irene y. lee & vc's clayton cowles
production

manny mederos
logo design

devin lewis
assistant editor

sana amanat
editor

nick lowe
senior editor

axel alonso
editor in chief

joe quesada
chief creative officer

dan buckley
publisher

alan fine
executive producer

SPECIAL THANKS TO STEPHEN WACKER

MARVEL
marvelkids.com

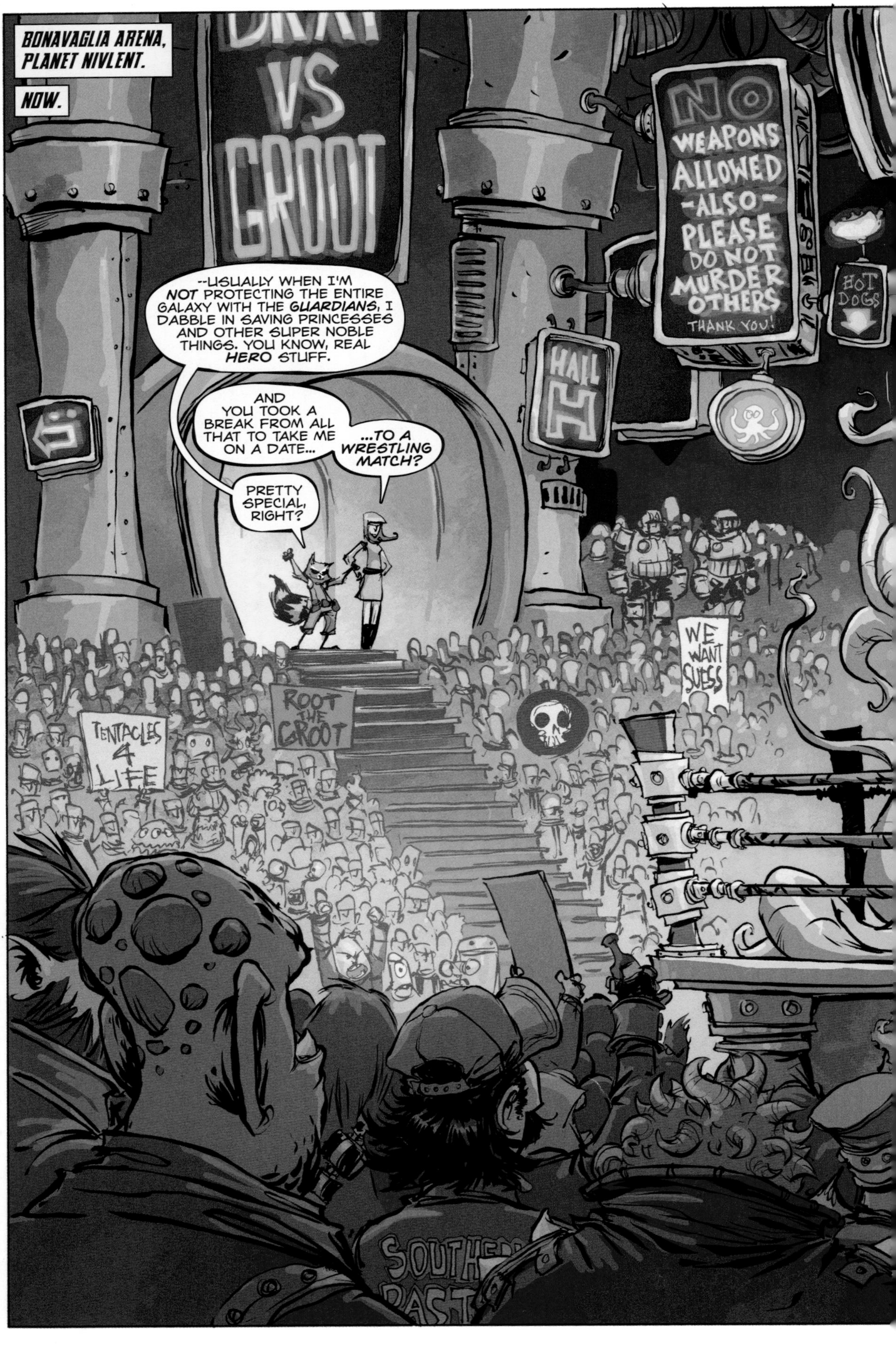

BONAVAGLIA ARENA, PLANET NIVLENT.
NOW.
VS GROOT
NO WEAPONS ALLOWED -ALSO- PLEASE DO NOT MURDER OTHERS THANK YOU!
HOT DOGS
HALL H
--USUALLY WHEN I'M NOT PROTECTING THE ENTIRE GALAXY WITH THE GUARDIANS, I DABBLE IN SAVING PRINCESSES AND OTHER SUPER NOBLE THINGS. YOU KNOW, REAL HERO STUFF.
AND YOU TOOK A BREAK FROM ALL THAT TO TAKE ME ON A DATE...
...TO A WRESTLING MATCH?
PRETTY SPECIAL, RIGHT?
WE WANT SUESS
ROOT THE GROOT
TENTACLES 4 LIFE

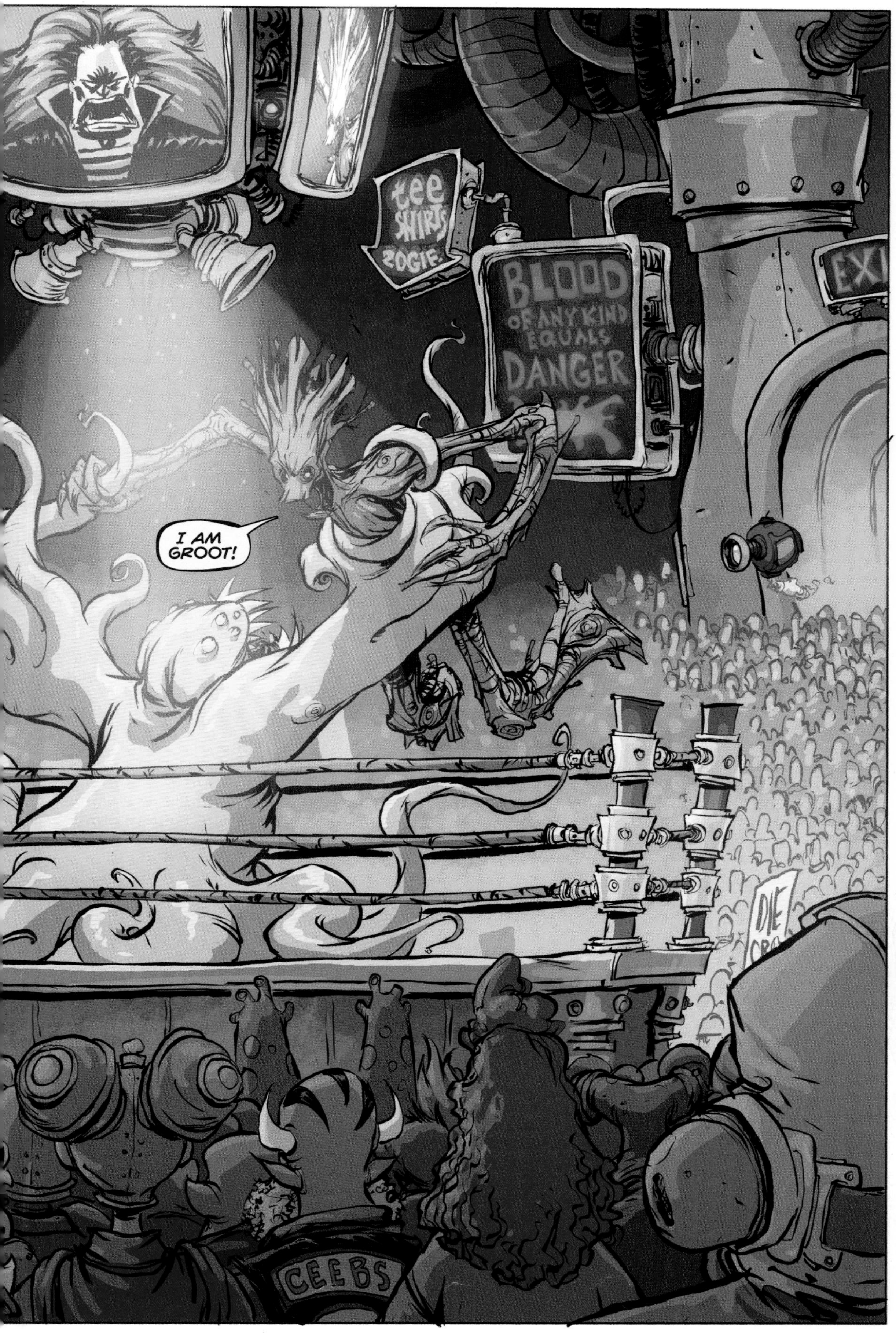
tee SHIRTS ZOGIE.
BLOOD OF ANY KIND EQUALS DANGER
I AM GROOT!
CEEBS

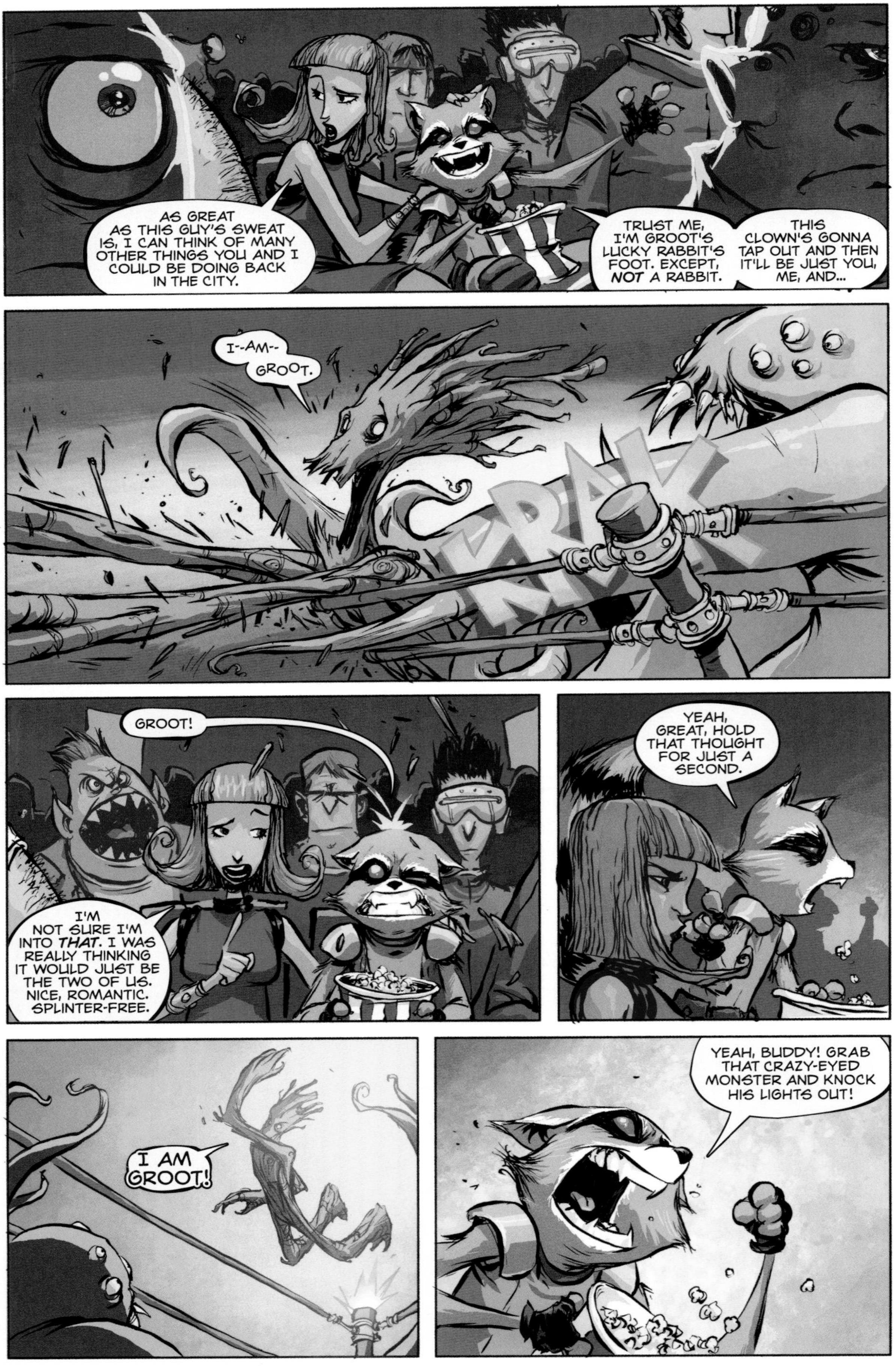

AS GREAT AS THIS GUY'S SWEAT IS, I CAN THINK OF MANY OTHER THINGS YOU AND I COULD BE DOING BACK IN THE CITY.
TRUST ME, I'M GROOT'S LUCKY RABBIT'S FOOT. EXCEPT, NOT A RABBIT.
THIS CLOWN'S GONNA TAP OUT AND THEN IT'LL BE JUST YOU, ME, AND...
I--AM--GROOT.
KRAK
GROOT!
I'M NOT SURE I'M INTO THAT. I WAS REALLY THINKING IT WOULD JUST BE THE TWO OF US. NICE, ROMANTIC. SPLINTER-FREE.
YEAH, GREAT, HOLD THAT THOUGHT FOR JUST A SECOND.
I AM GROOT!
YEAH, BUDDY! GRAB THAT CRAZY-EYED MONSTER AND KNOCK HIS LIGHTS OUT!

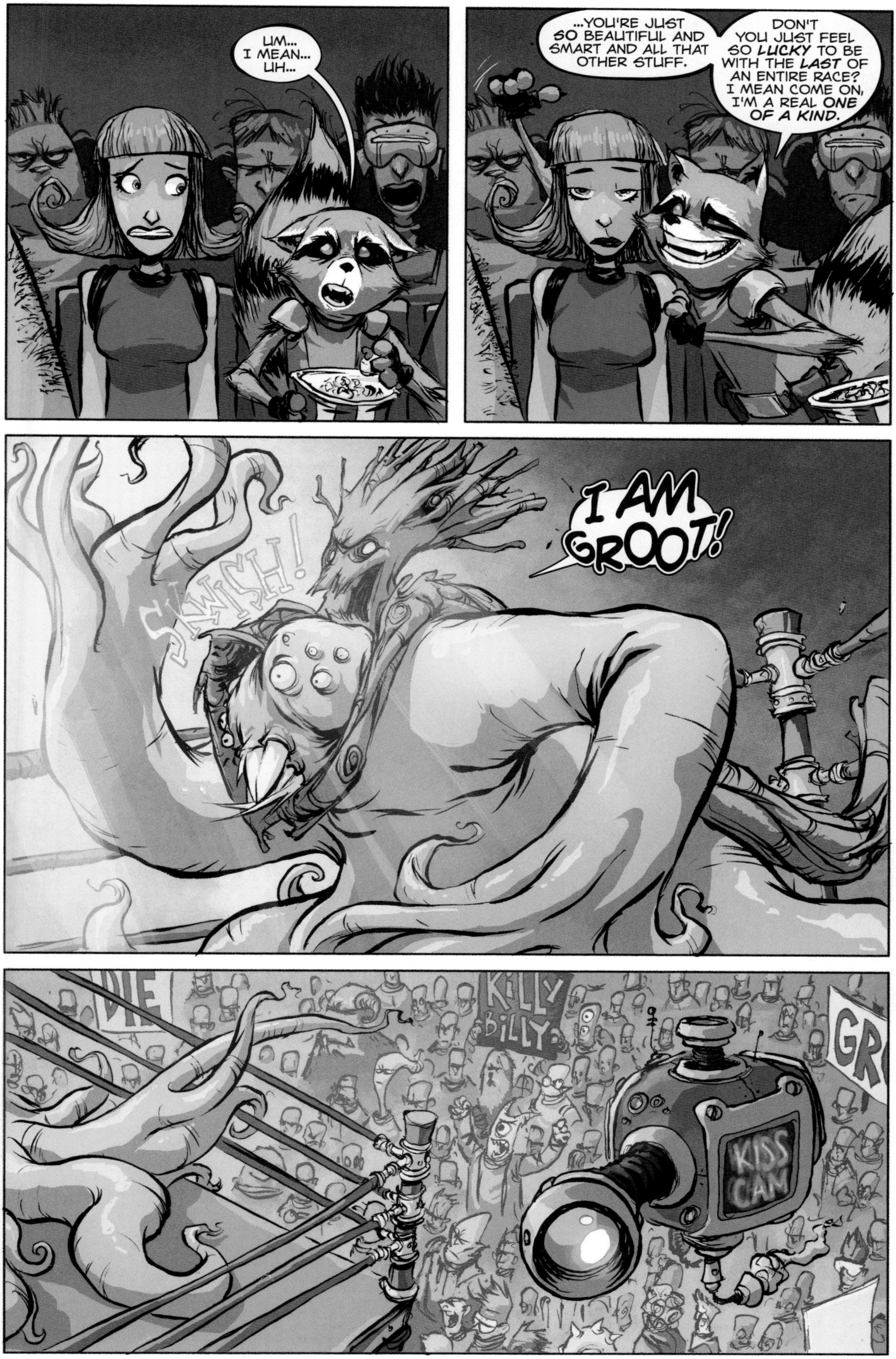
UM... I MEAN... UH...
...YOU'RE JUST SO BEAUTIFUL AND SMART AND ALL THAT OTHER STUFF.
DON'T YOU JUST FEEL SO LUCKY TO BE WITH THE LAST OF AN ENTIRE RACE? I MEAN COME ON, I'M A REAL ONE OF A KIND.
SWISH!
I AM GROOT!
DIE
KILLY BILLY
KISS CAM

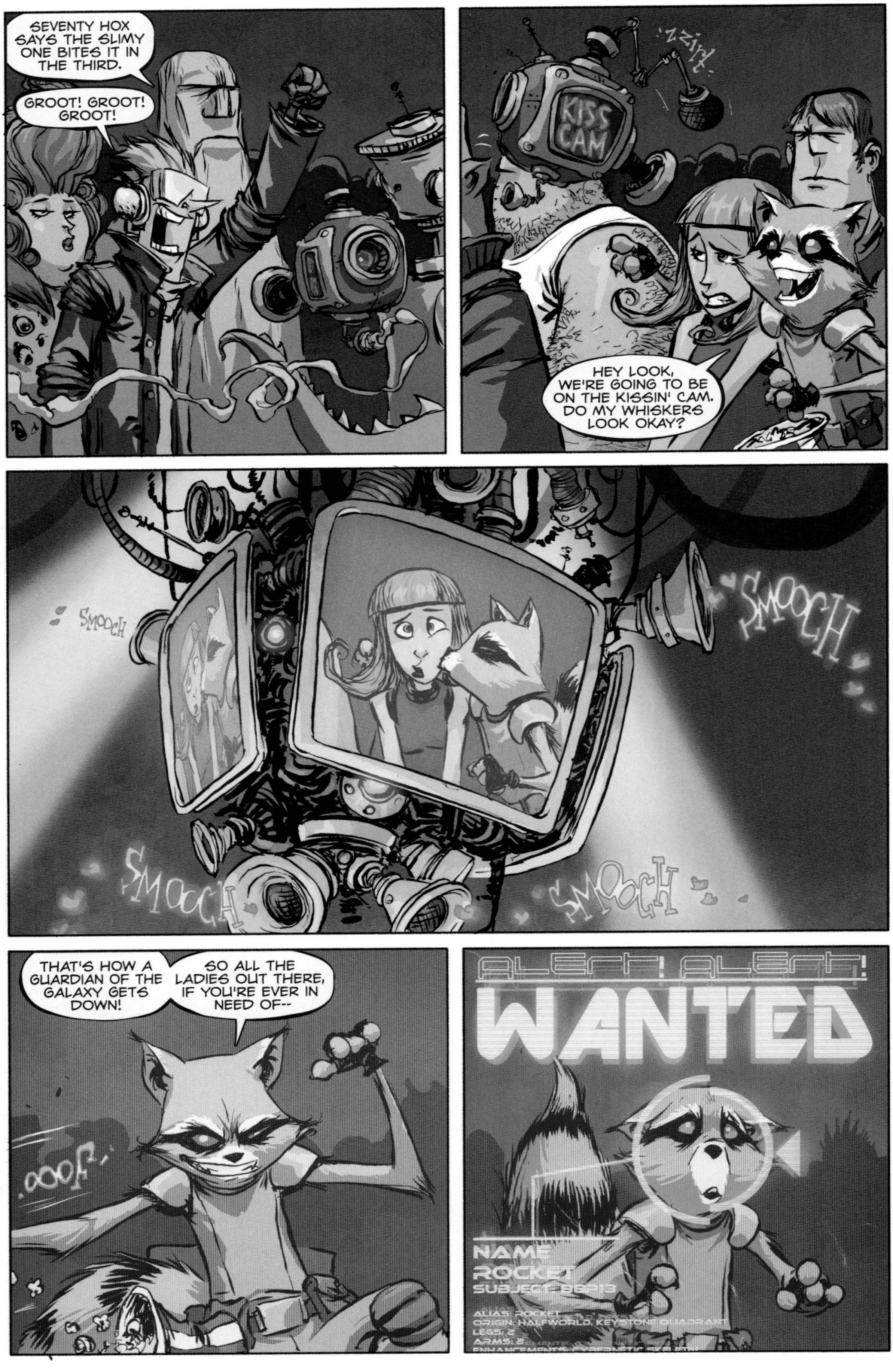
SEVENTY HOX SAYS THE SLIMY ONE BITES IT IN THE THIRD.
GROOT! GROOT! GROOT!
ZZIRT
KISS CAM
HEY LOOK, WE'RE GOING TO BE ON THE KISSIN' CAM. DO MY WHISKERS LOOK OKAY?
SMOOCH
SMOOCH
SMOOCH
SMOOCH
THAT'S HOW A GUARDIAN OF THE GALAXY GETS DOWN!
SO ALL THE LADIES OUT THERE, IF YOU'RE EVER IN NEED OF--
OOOF!
ALERT! ALERT!
WANTED
NAME
ROCKET
SUBJECT 89P13
ALIAS: ROCKET
ORIGIN: HALFWORLD, KEYSTONE QUADRANT
LEGS: 2
ARMS: 2

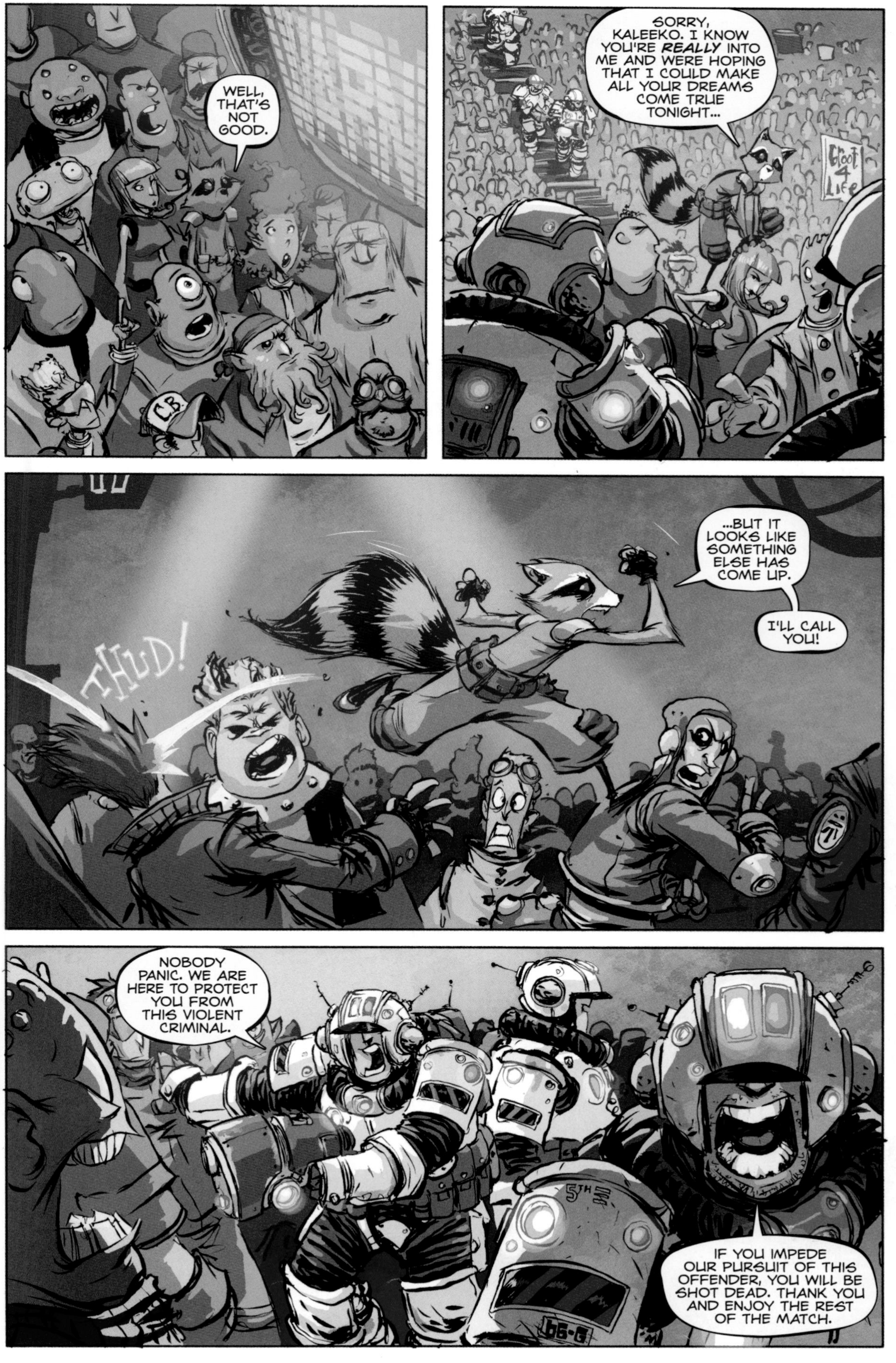
WELL, THAT'S NOT GOOD.
SORRY, KALEEKO. I KNOW YOU'RE *REALLY* INTO ME AND WERE HOPING THAT I COULD MAKE ALL YOUR DREAMS COME TRUE TONIGHT...
Groot 4 Life
...BUT IT LOOKS LIKE SOMETHING ELSE HAS COME UP.
I'LL CALL YOU!
THUD!
NOBODY PANIC. WE ARE HERE TO PROTECT YOU FROM THIS VIOLENT CRIMINAL.
IF YOU IMPEDE OUR PURSUIT OF THIS OFFENDER, YOU WILL BE SHOT DEAD. THANK YOU AND ENJOY THE REST OF THE MATCH.

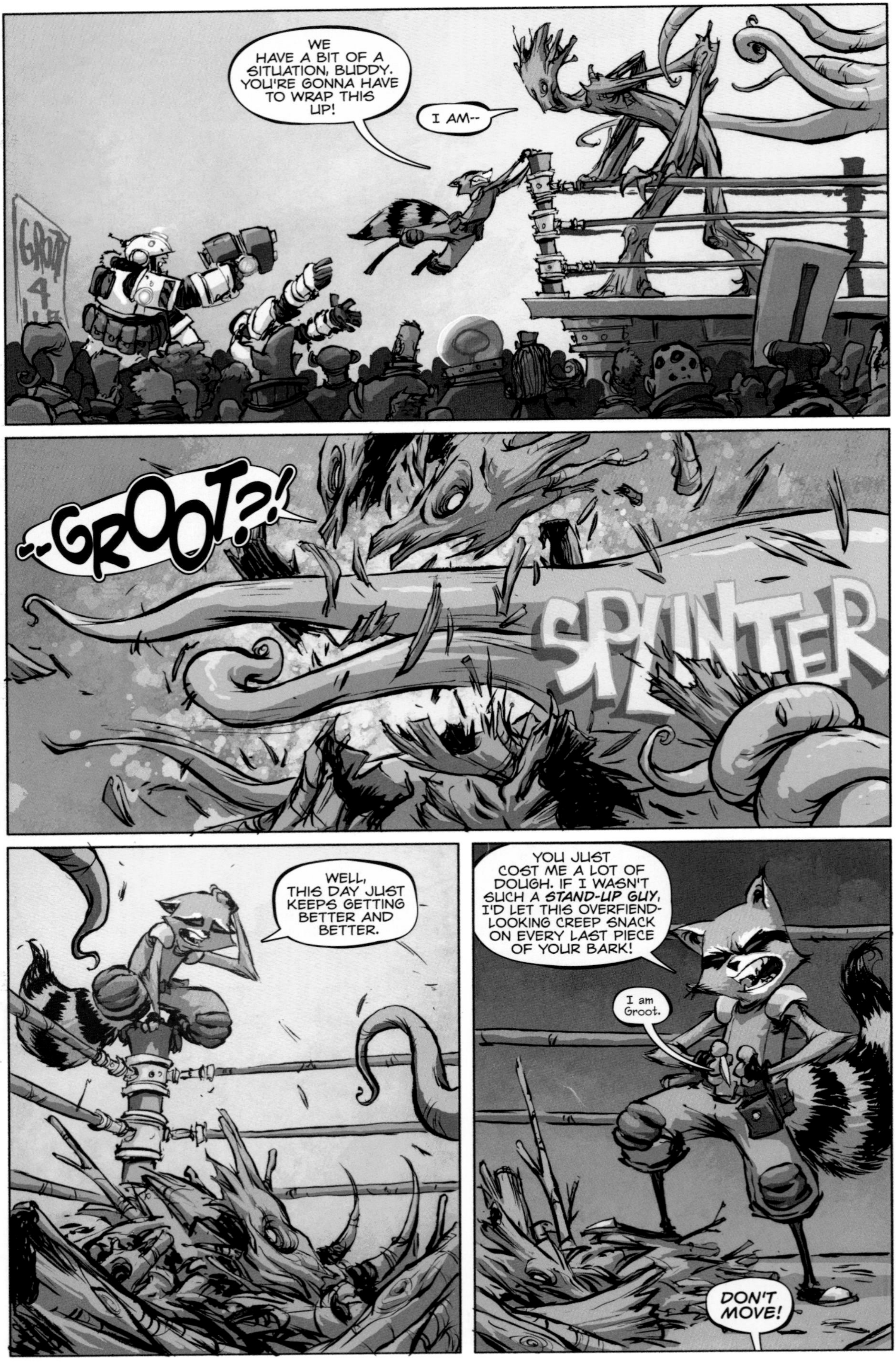
WE HAVE A BIT OF A SITUATION, BUDDY. YOU'RE GONNA HAVE TO WRAP THIS UP!
I AM--
--GROOT?!
SPLINTER
WELL, THIS DAY JUST KEEPS GETTING BETTER AND BETTER.
YOU JUST COST ME A LOT OF DOUGH. IF I WASN'T SUCH A *STAND-UP GUY*, I'D LET THIS OVERFIEND-LOOKING CREEP SNACK ON EVERY LAST PIECE OF YOUR BARK!
I am Groot.
DON'T MOVE!

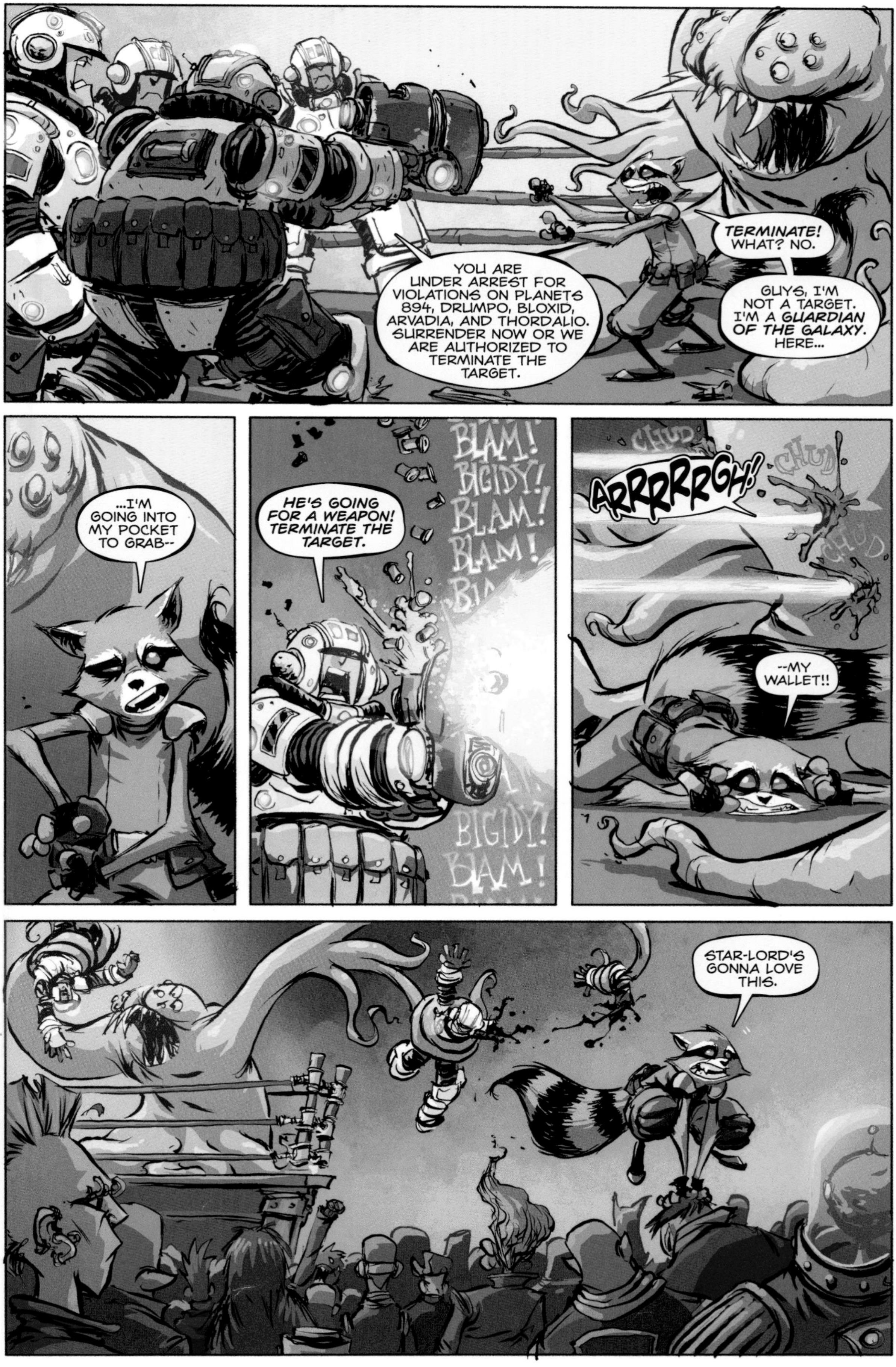
YOU ARE UNDER ARREST FOR VIOLATIONS ON PLANETS 894, DRUMPO, BLOXID, ARVADIA, AND THORDALIO. SURRENDER NOW OR WE ARE AUTHORIZED TO TERMINATE THE TARGET.
TERMINATE! WHAT? NO.
GUYS, I'M NOT A TARGET. I'M A GUARDIAN OF THE GALAXY. HERE...
...I'M GOING INTO MY POCKET TO GRAB--
HE'S GOING FOR A WEAPON! TERMINATE THE TARGET.
BLAM! BIGIDY! BLAM! BLAM!
BIGIDY! BLAM!
CHUD
ARRRRRGH!
CHUD
CHUD
--MY WALLET!!
STAR-LORD'S GONNA LOVE THIS.

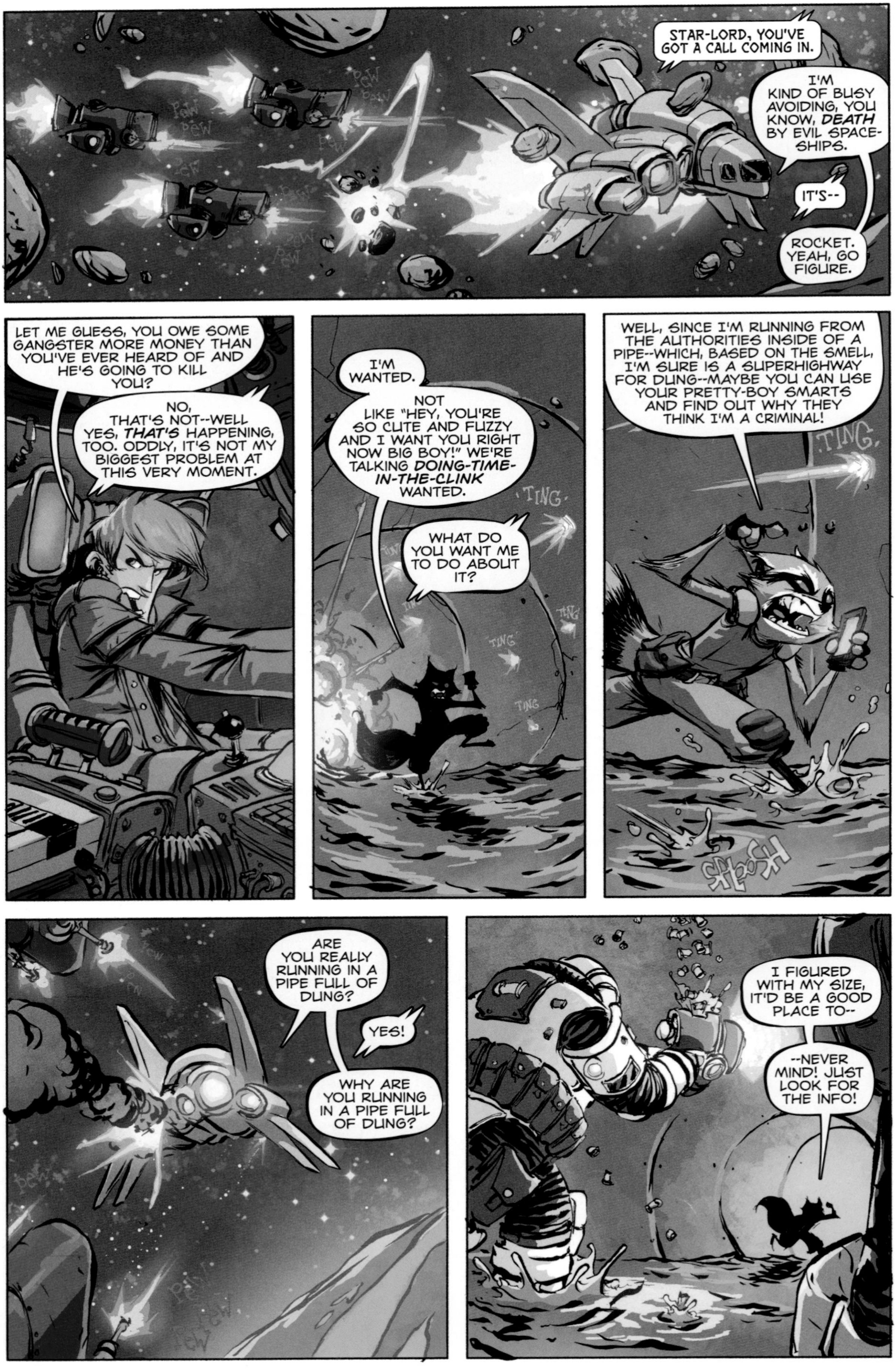
STAR-LORD, YOU'VE GOT A CALL COMING IN.
I'M KIND OF BUSY AVOIDING, YOU KNOW, *DEATH* BY EVIL SPACE-SHIPS.
IT'S--
ROCKET. YEAH, GO FIGURE.
PEW PEW
LET ME GUESS, YOU OWE SOME GANGSTER MORE MONEY THAN YOU'VE EVER HEARD OF AND HE'S GOING TO KILL YOU?
NO, THAT'S NOT--WELL YES, *THAT'S* HAPPENING, TOO. ODDLY, IT'S NOT MY BIGGEST PROBLEM AT THIS VERY MOMENT.
I'M WANTED.
NOT LIKE "HEY, YOU'RE SO CUTE AND FUZZY AND I WANT YOU RIGHT NOW BIG BOY!" WE'RE TALKING *DOING-TIME-IN-THE-CLINK* WANTED.
WHAT DO YOU WANT ME TO DO ABOUT IT?
TING
WELL, SINCE I'M RUNNING FROM THE AUTHORITIES INSIDE OF A PIPE--WHICH, BASED ON THE SMELL, I'M SURE IS A SUPERHIGHWAY FOR DUNG--MAYBE YOU CAN USE YOUR PRETTY-BOY SMARTS AND FIND OUT WHY THEY THINK I'M A CRIMINAL!
TING
ARE YOU REALLY RUNNING IN A PIPE FULL OF DUNG?
YES!
WHY ARE YOU RUNNING IN A PIPE FULL OF DUNG?
I FIGURED WITH MY SIZE, IT'D BE A GOOD PLACE TO--
--NEVER MIND! JUST LOOK FOR THE INFO!

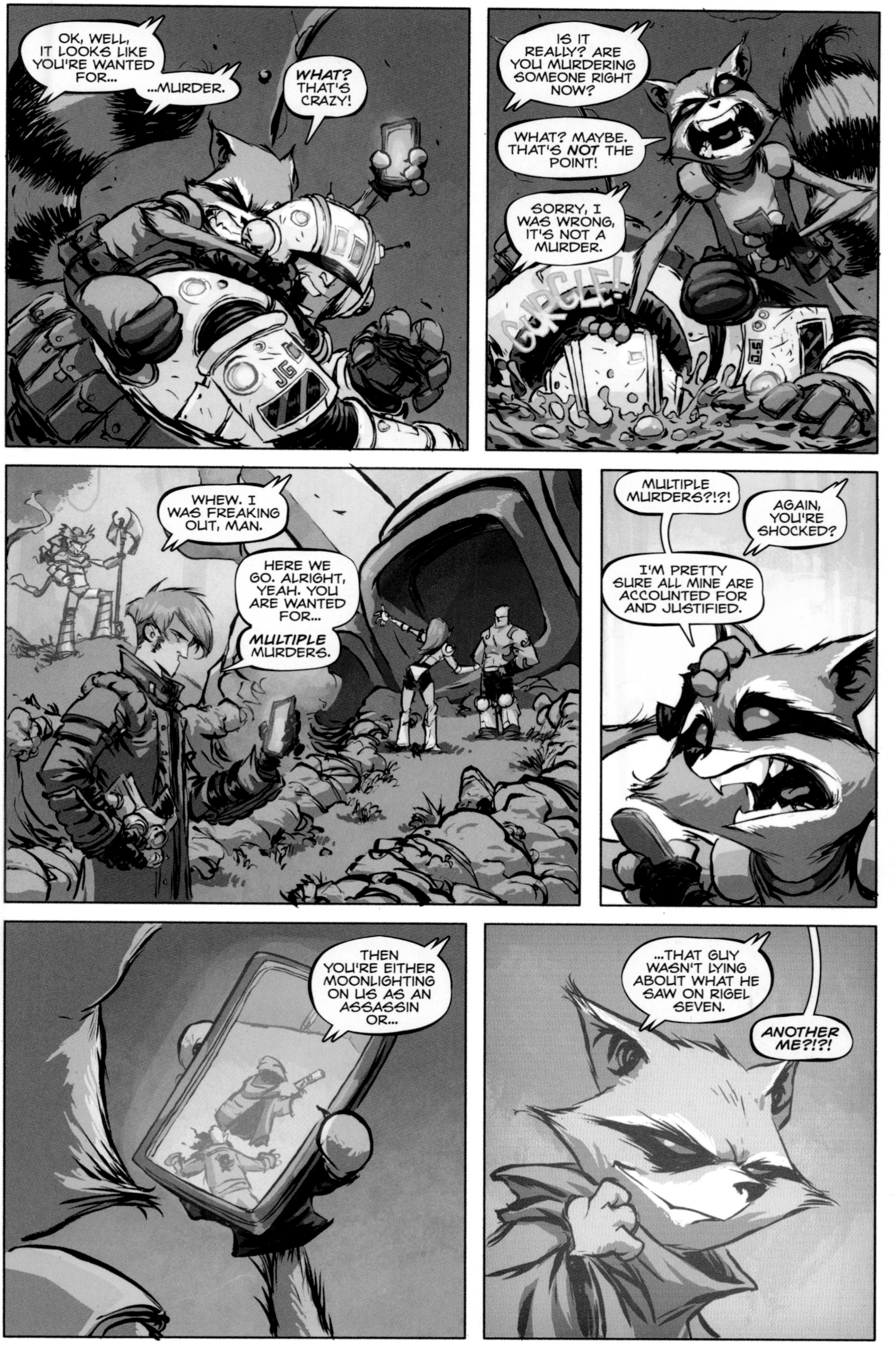
OK, WELL, IT LOOKS LIKE YOU'RE WANTED FOR...
...MURDER.
WHAT? THAT'S CRAZY!
IS IT REALLY? ARE YOU MURDERING SOMEONE RIGHT NOW?
WHAT? MAYBE. THAT'S *NOT* THE POINT!
SORRY, I WAS WRONG, IT'S NOT A MURDER.
GURGLE!
WHEW. I WAS FREAKING OUT, MAN.
HERE WE GO. ALRIGHT, YEAH. YOU ARE WANTED FOR...
MULTIPLE MURDERS.
MULTIPLE MURDERS?!?!
AGAIN, YOU'RE SHOCKED?
I'M PRETTY SURE ALL MINE ARE ACCOUNTED FOR AND JUSTIFIED.
THEN YOU'RE EITHER MOONLIGHTING ON US AS AN ASSASSIN OR...
...THAT GUY WASN'T LYING ABOUT WHAT HE SAW ON RIGEL SEVEN.
ANOTHER ME?!?!

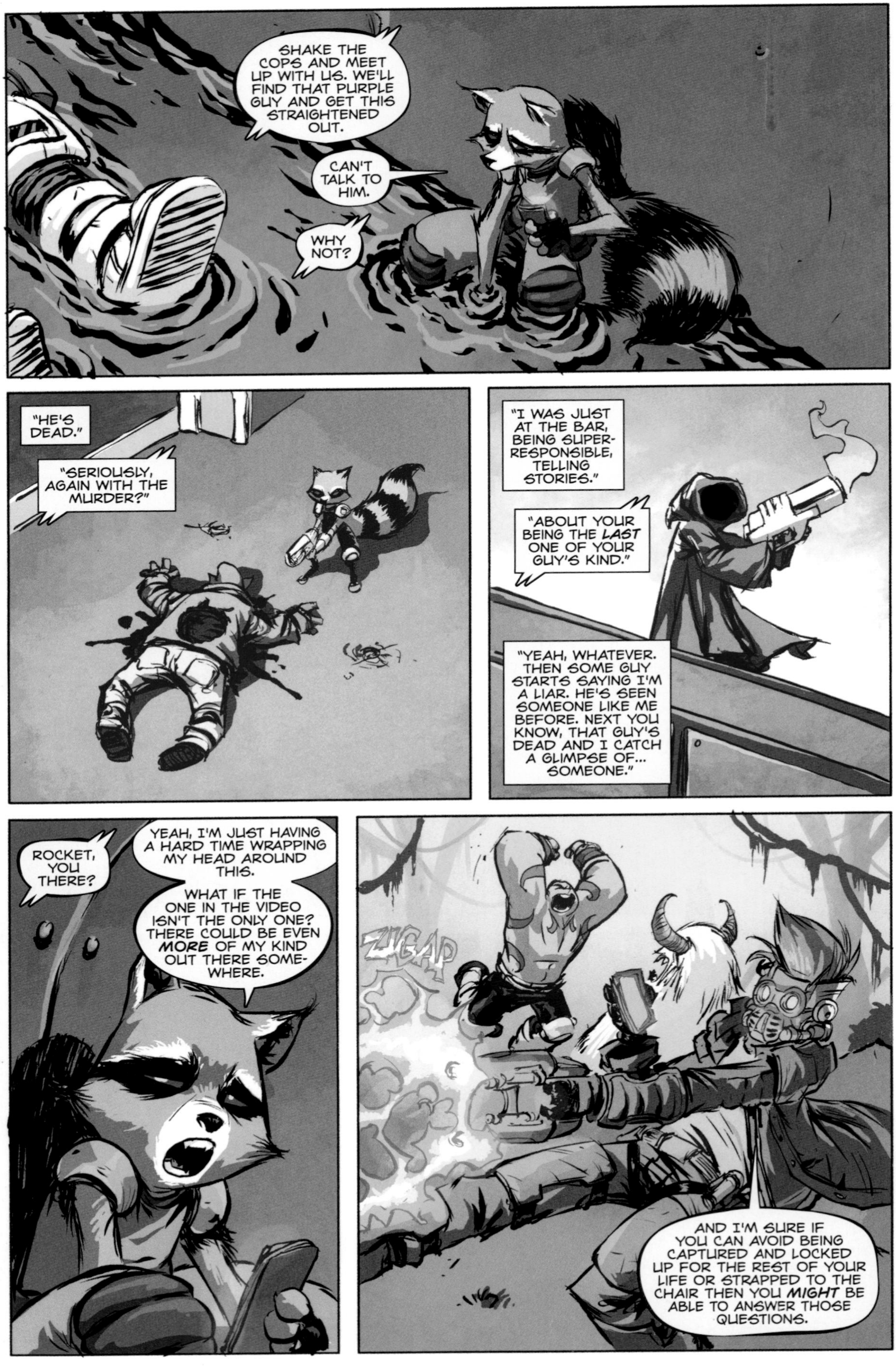
SHAKE THE COPS AND MEET UP WITH US. WE'LL FIND THAT PURPLE GUY AND GET THIS STRAIGHTENED OUT.
CAN'T TALK TO HIM.
WHY NOT?
"HE'S DEAD."
"SERIOUSLY, AGAIN WITH THE MURDER?"
"I WAS JUST AT THE BAR, BEING SUPER-RESPONSIBLE, TELLING STORIES."
"ABOUT YOUR BEING THE ***LAST*** ONE OF YOUR GUY'S KIND."
"YEAH, WHATEVER. THEN SOME GUY STARTS SAYING I'M A LIAR. HE'S SEEN SOMEONE LIKE ME BEFORE. NEXT YOU KNOW, THAT GUY'S DEAD AND I CATCH A GLIMPSE OF... SOMEONE."
ROCKET, YOU THERE?
YEAH, I'M JUST HAVING A HARD TIME WRAPPING MY HEAD AROUND THIS.
WHAT IF THE ONE IN THE VIDEO ISN'T THE ONLY ONE? THERE COULD BE EVEN ***MORE*** OF MY KIND OUT THERE SOMEWHERE.
ZZGAP
AND I'M SURE IF YOU CAN AVOID BEING CAPTURED AND LOCKED UP FOR THE REST OF YOUR LIFE OR STRAPPED TO THE CHAIR THEN YOU ***MIGHT*** BE ABLE TO ANSWER THOSE QUESTIONS.

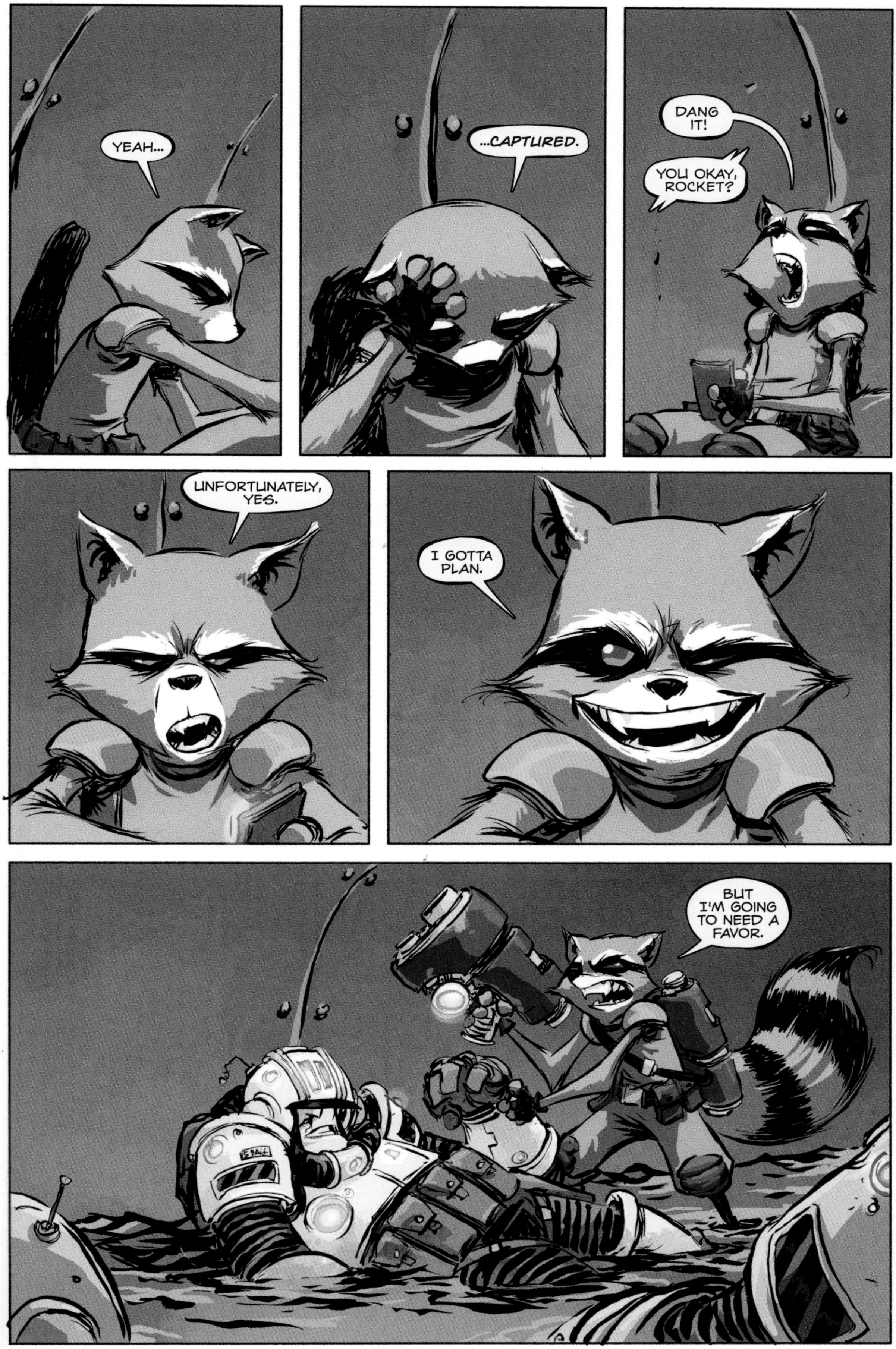
YEAH...
...CAPTURED.
DANG IT!
YOU OKAY, ROCKET?
UNFORTUNATELY, YES.
I GOTTA PLAN.
BUT I'M GOING TO NEED A FAVOR.

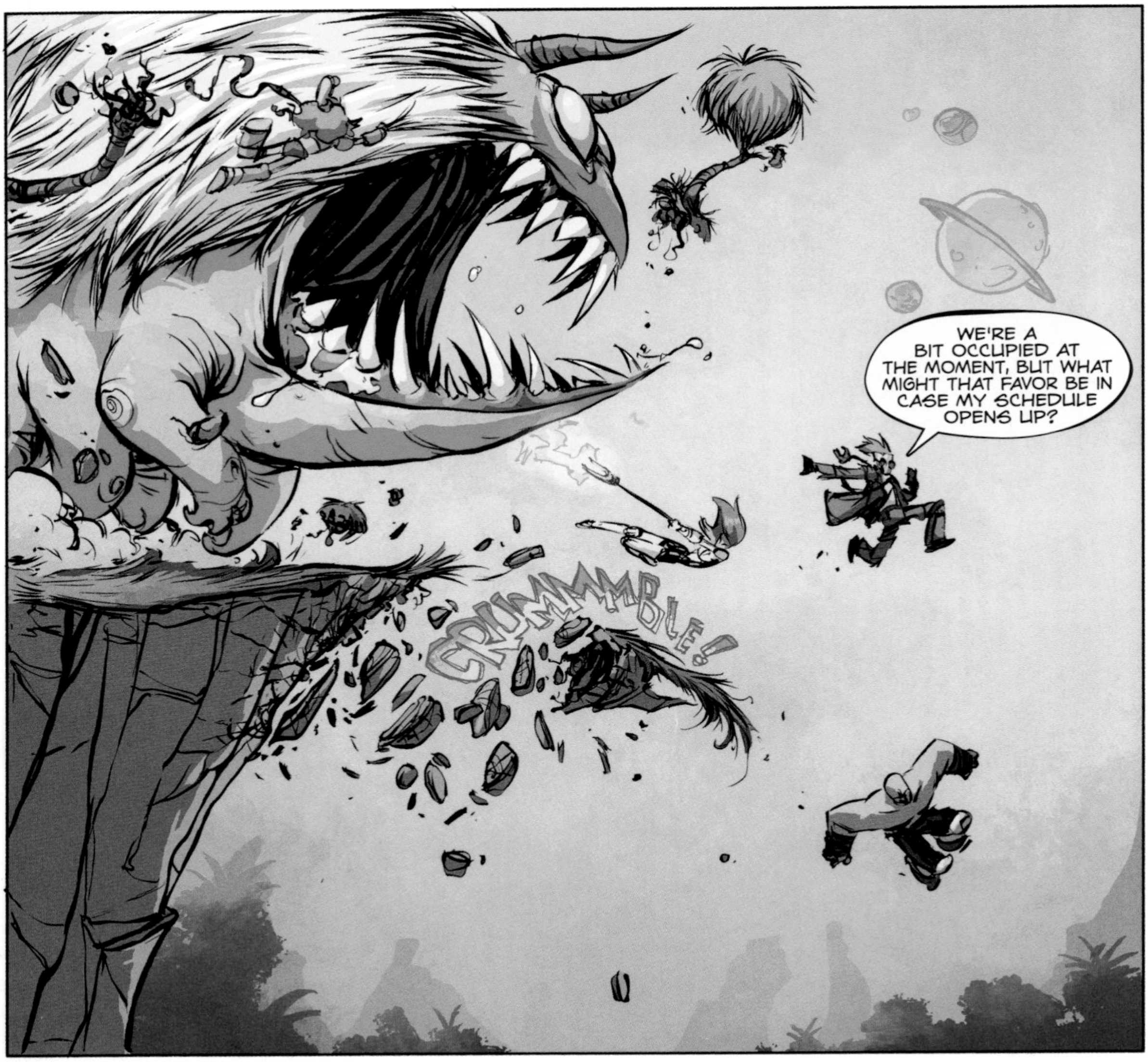
WE'RE A BIT OCCUPIED AT THE MOMENT, BUT WHAT MIGHT THAT FAVOR BE IN CASE MY SCHEDULE OPENS UP?
CRUMMMBLE!

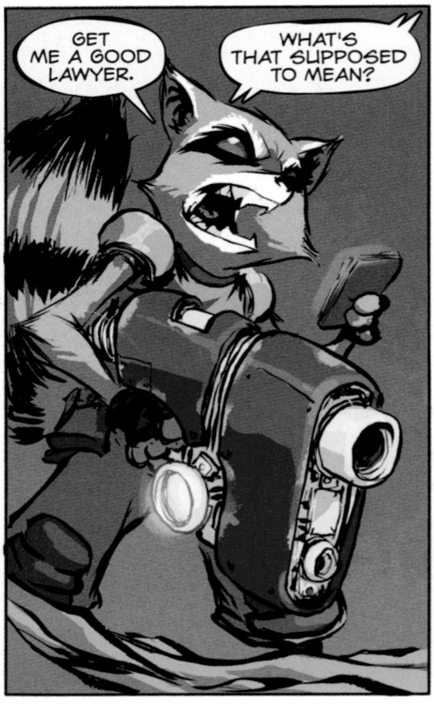
GET ME A GOOD LAWYER.
WHAT'S THAT SUPPOSED TO MEAN?

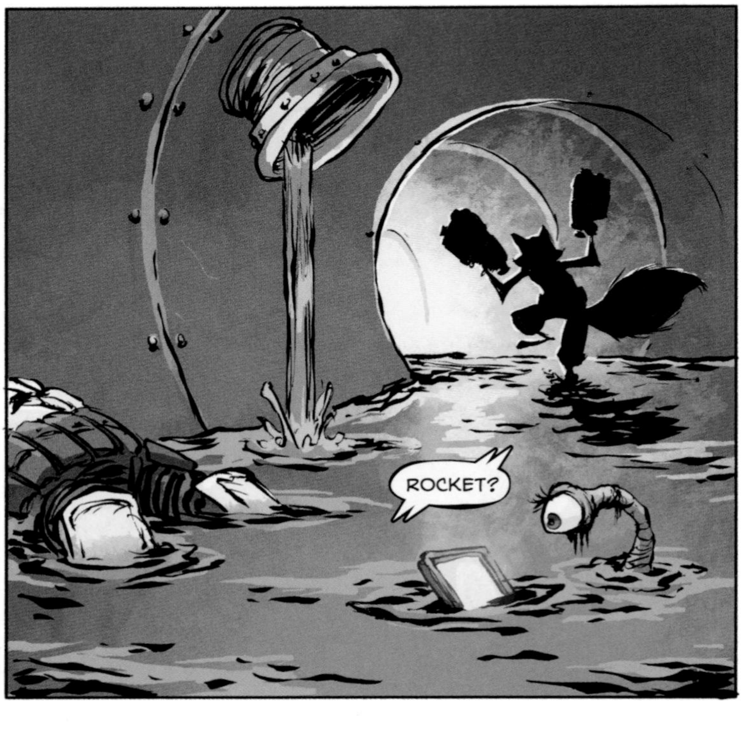
ROCKET?

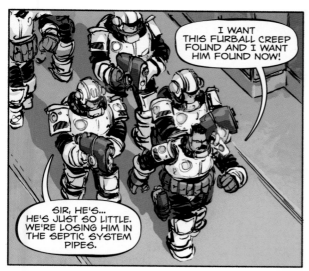

I WANT THIS FURBALL CREEP FOUND AND I WANT HIM FOUND NOW!

SIR, HE'S... HE'S JUST SO LITTLE. WE'RE LOSING HIM IN THE SEPTIC SYSTEM PIPES.

I DON'T CARE IF HE'S SMALL ENOUGH TO CRAWL INTO YOUR EAR!

CLONK!

NOW, SEEING AS YOU ALL ARE THE AUTHORITIES AND I'M *MOSTLY* A LAW-ABIDING CITIZEN AND ALL-AROUND NICE GUY...

I'VE DECIDED TO MAKE YOUR JOBS A LITTLE EASIER.

WHAT THE--

MMMMM DROP!

I'D LIKE TO BE ARRESTED, PLEASE, AND TAKEN IN FOR QUESTIONING. THANKS.

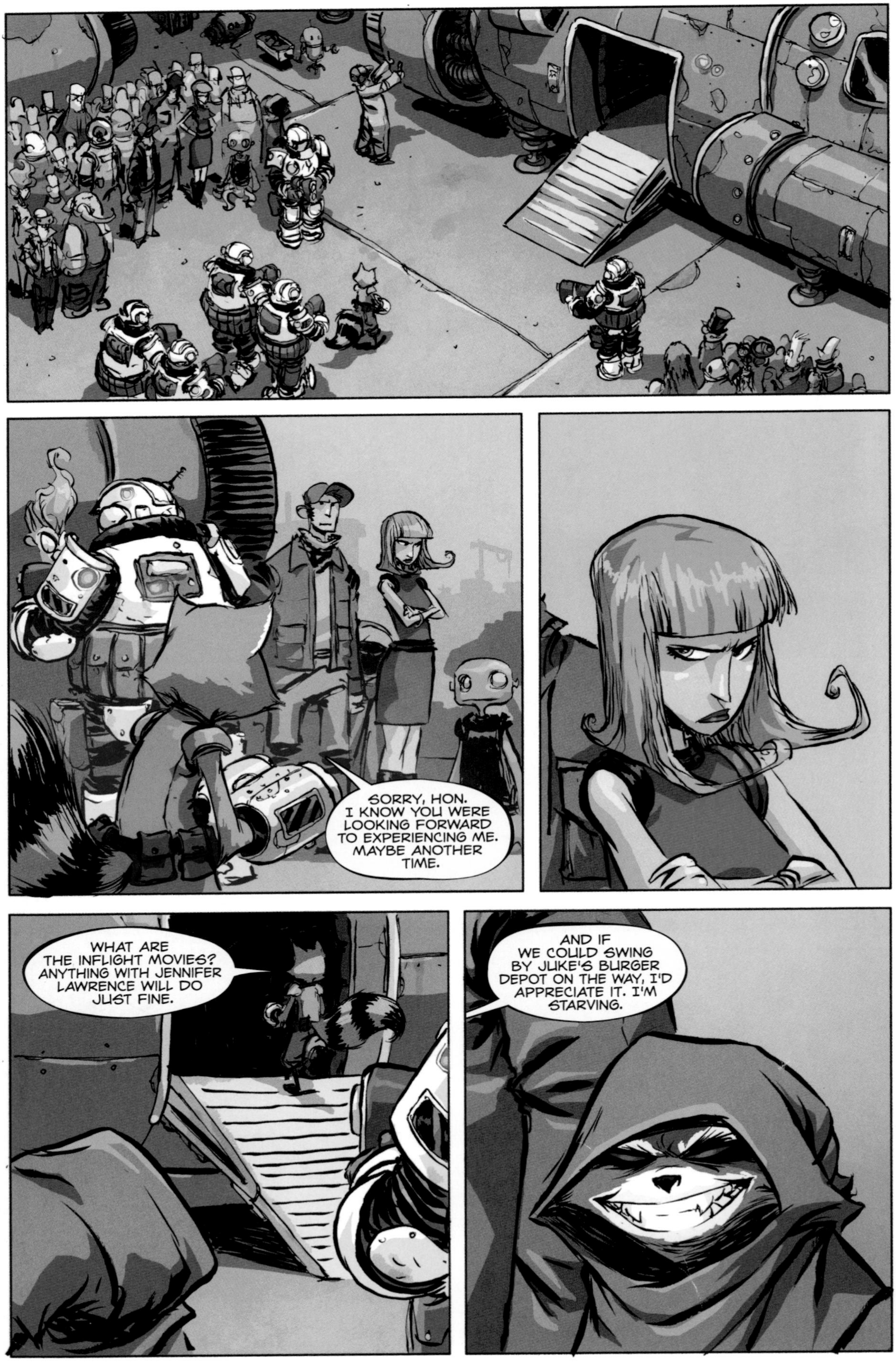
SORRY, HON. I KNOW YOU WERE LOOKING FORWARD TO EXPERIENCING ME. MAYBE ANOTHER TIME.
WHAT ARE THE INFLIGHT MOVIES? ANYTHING WITH JENNIFER LAWRENCE WILL DO JUST FINE.
AND IF WE COULD SWING BY JUKE'S BURGER DEPOT ON THE WAY, I'D APPRECIATE IT. I'M STARVING.

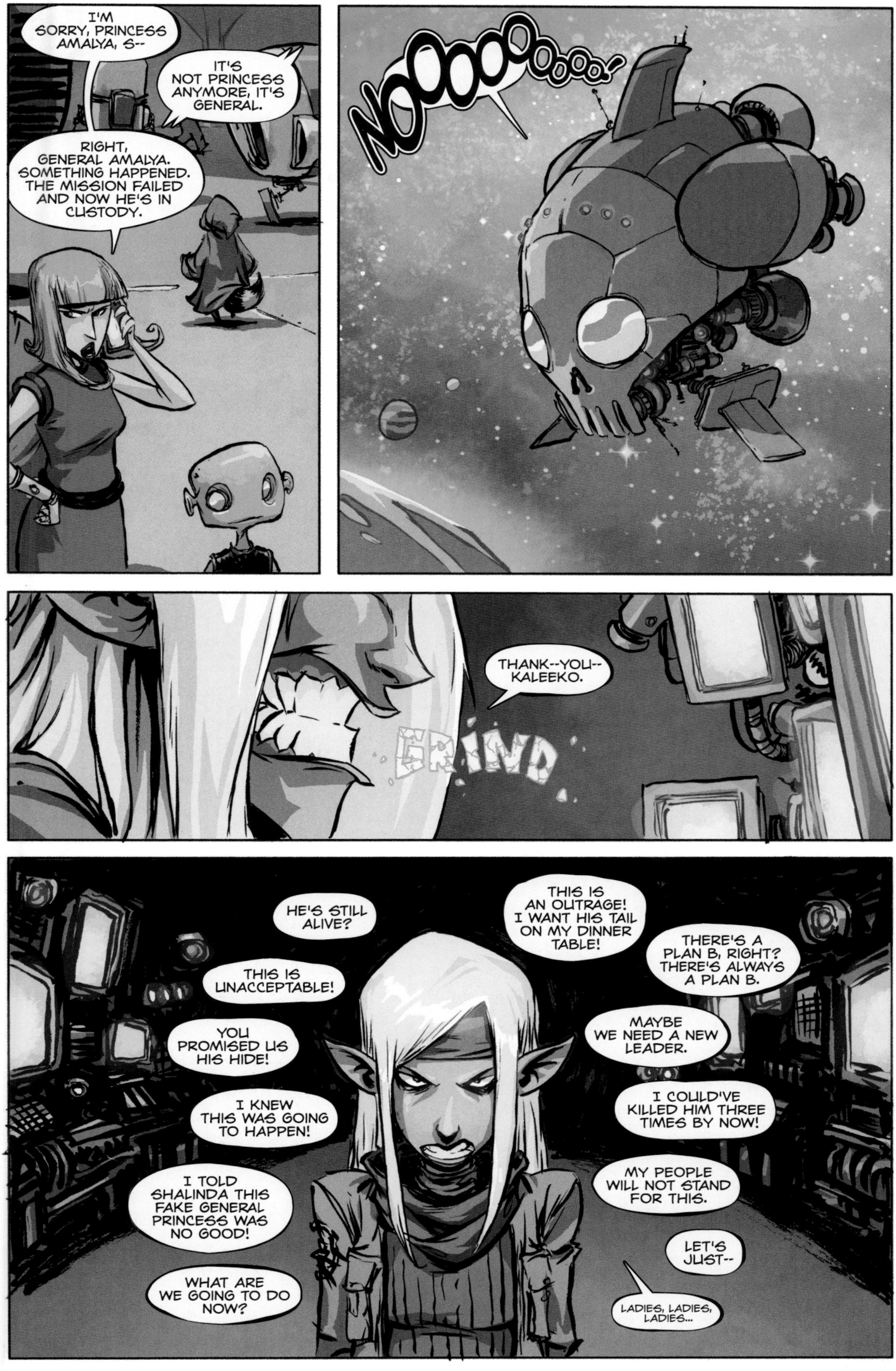
I'M SORRY, PRINCESS AMALYA, S--
IT'S NOT PRINCESS ANYMORE, IT'S GENERAL.
RIGHT, GENERAL AMALYA. SOMETHING HAPPENED. THE MISSION FAILED AND NOW HE'S IN CUSTODY.
NOOOOOoooo!
THANK--YOU--KALEEKO.
GRIND
HE'S STILL ALIVE?
THIS IS UNACCEPTABLE!
YOU PROMISED US HIS HIDE!
I KNEW THIS WAS GOING TO HAPPEN!
I TOLD SHALINDA THIS FAKE GENERAL PRINCESS WAS NO GOOD!
WHAT ARE WE GOING TO DO NOW?
THIS IS AN OUTRAGE! I WANT HIS TAIL ON MY DINNER TABLE!
THERE'S A PLAN B, RIGHT? THERE'S ALWAYS A PLAN B.
MAYBE WE NEED A NEW LEADER.
I COULD'VE KILLED HIM THREE TIMES BY NOW!
MY PEOPLE WILL NOT STAND FOR THIS.
LET'S JUST--
LADIES, LADIES, LADIES...

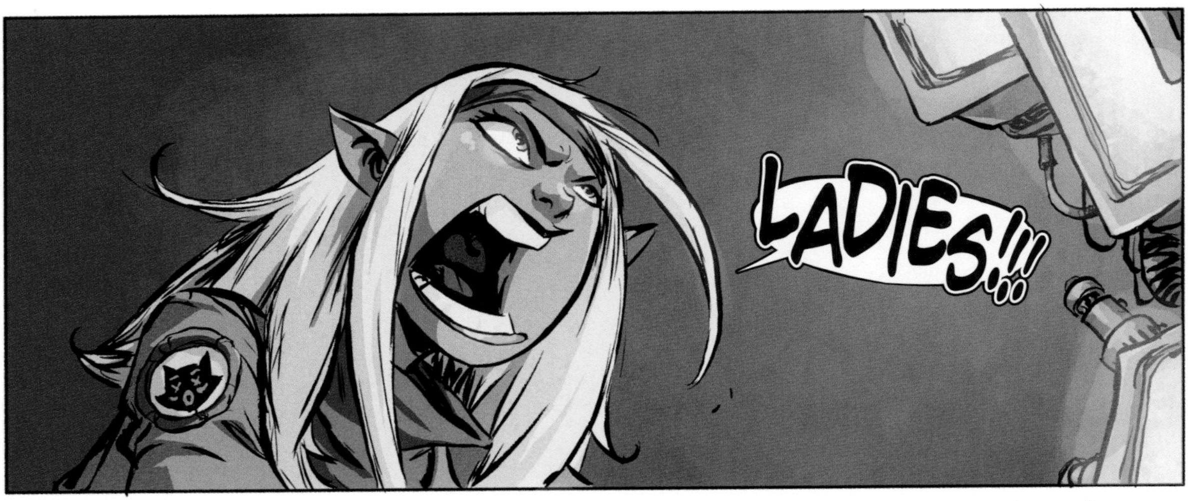
LADIES!!!

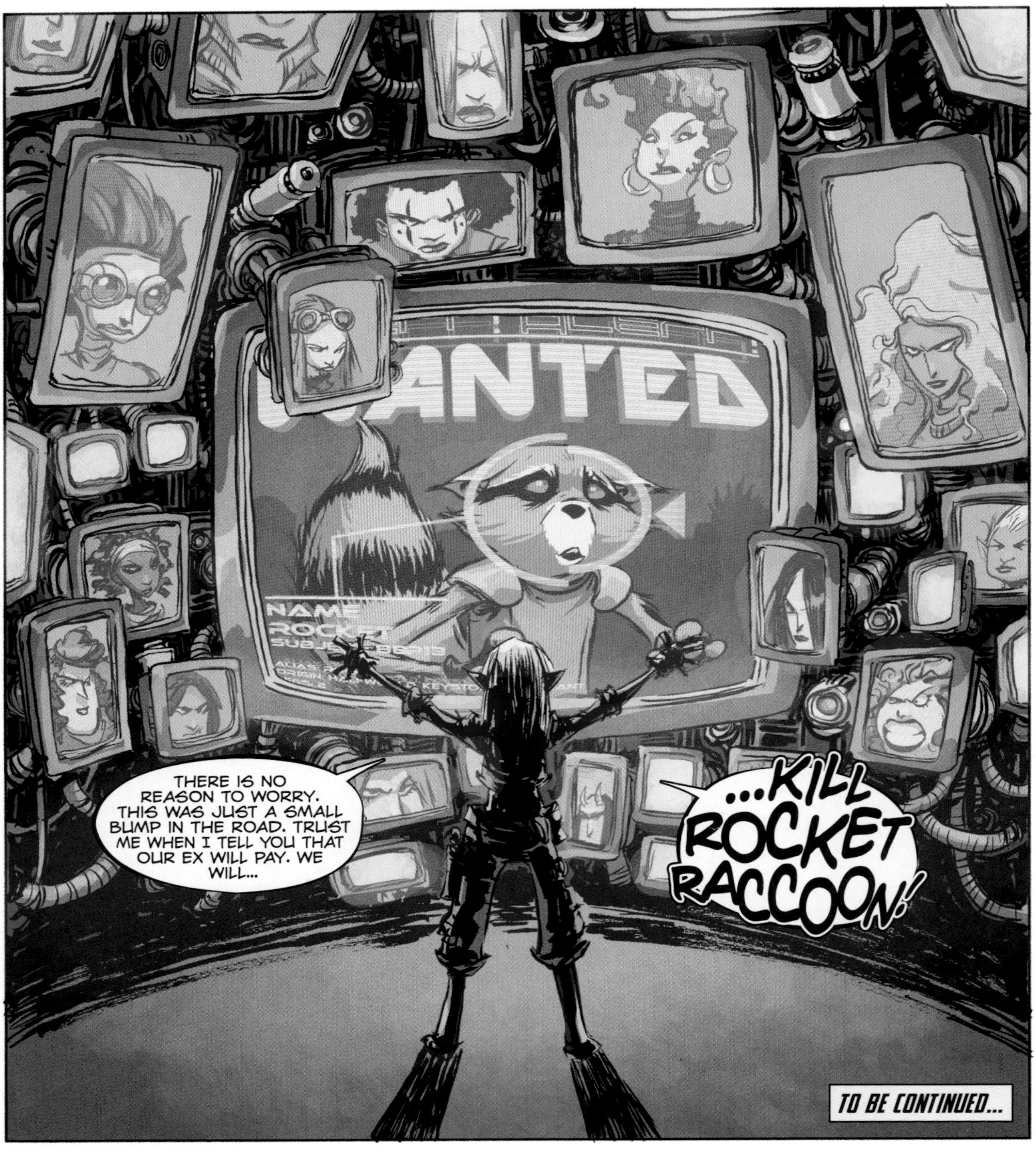
NAME
THERE IS NO REASON TO WORRY. THIS WAS JUST A SMALL BUMP IN THE ROAD. TRUST ME WHEN I TELL YOU THAT OUR EX WILL PAY. WE WILL...
...KILL ROCKET RACCOON!
TO BE CONTINUED...